The White Mouse

A tale from the Panchatantra

Retold by Dawn Casey

Illustrated by Masako Masukawa

Collins

Chapter 1

In the foothills of the Himalaya Mountains, a blue-green river rippled over the rocks and sparkled in the sunshine. On the banks of the river lived an old man and his wife.

The old man had spent his years studying ancient books.
He was so wise, he'd developed magical powers. But there was
one thing the old man didn't have. He and his wife had always
wanted a child, but they had neither son nor daughter.

One day, when the old
man was washing his
face in the river,
a falcon flew overhead.
In its claws was
a white mouse.
The mouse wriggled
and, for a moment,
the falcon loosened its grip.
With a squeak, the little mouse fell
to earth.

The old man looked up
and saw the great
bird, and he saw
the mouse falling.

Quickly, he stretched out
his hands and caught her.
The corners of his eyes
crinkled with delight as
he spoke. "Hello, little one,"
he said. "Don't be afraid."

"Look!" the old man called to his wife. "This young mouse escaped from a falcon! She has no family, no home."

The old woman looked at him with hope in her eyes. "We can help her, can't we?"

The old man smiled. "Yes," he said. "Yes, we can."

Then, as his wife watched in wonder, he began to perform powerful magic. He lifted his brass water pot. It was filled with water from the bright river which connects the great mountain to the vast sea. The old man dipped his fingertips into the pot and gently sprinkled the mouse with water. The water sparkled around her like droplets of light.

Then the old man closed his eyes and began to chant ...

6

Chapter 2

When the old man opened his eyes, the little mouse had changed.
She was now a little girl, with dark hair and bright eyes.

The old woman knelt down to her. "Dear child," she said.
"We'll give you all you need. We'll love you like our own daughter."
The girl smiled and the old woman's eyes filled with happy tears.

The old woman prepared the most delicious meals for
her new daughter. She sewed her saris of green and gold,
and scarves of silver and scarlet.

The old man told the girl stories he'd heard when he was a boy.
The tales the girl loved best were about animals – the wise lion
and the clever monkey, and the kind-hearted hare who lives on
the moon.

At dawn, they went swimming and splashing in the cold, clear
water of the river. At dusk, they wove together leaves and
twigs to make tiny boats. The girl filled them with flowers and
candles, then set them sailing on the water. She loved to watch
them floating on the river, glowing with light.

The years passed and the girl grew.

Early one morning, the old woman stood watching her daughter. "My dear," she said to her husband, "our daughter's a child no more."

The old man put his arm around his wife's shoulder. "Indeed," he replied. "She's grown into a young woman."

And so the family agreed that it was time for the girl to marry.
"I'll help you to find a husband," said the old man. "But, in
the end, you must choose by listening to your own heart."

Because the old couple loved their daughter more than
anything in the world, they wondered who on earth would be
good enough to marry her? Only the best, the greatest, the most
powerful husband in the world would do!

Chapter 3

The old man sat up all night, thinking about who would make the perfect husband for his daughter. In the morning, the sun rose over the hills, bringing warmth and light. And as the first golden rays of sun touched his face, he had a wonderful idea.

"The sun!" he cried. "No one's more powerful than the sun! *He* would be good enough for my daughter."

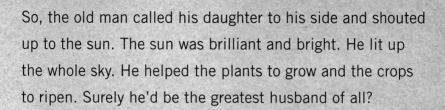

So, the old man called his daughter to his side and shouted up to the sun. The sun was brilliant and bright. He lit up the whole sky. He helped the plants to grow and the crops to ripen. Surely he'd be the greatest husband of all?

The girl knew her father was trying to help her, so she raised her face to look at the sun. But the sun's rays were so strong she had to cover her eyes. "I'm sorry, father," she said. "I don't want to marry the sun. He's too bright for me."

The old man squeezed his daughter's hand. He nodded. But who could be better than the sun? He called up, "Oh, radiant sun! Is there anyone on earth more powerful than you?"

The sun beamed down. "See how I shine! And yet, the cloud can always dim my light. The cloud's far more powerful than me."

"Where can we find the cloud?" asked the old man. The girl pointed and they both looked up, up, up, to the very top of the mountain.

The old man picked up his staff and his bundle of belongings, and the old woman handed the girl a tin of food for their journey.

"Do take care," she said. "There are bears in the forests and wolves in the hills. And the mountain is so high and the path is so narrow. It'll be difficult, it'll be dangerous …"

The girl grinned. "It'll be an adventure!"

14

Chapter 4

Together, the girl and her father walked the winding path up the mountain. The road rose higher and higher, until soon their green valley lay far below.

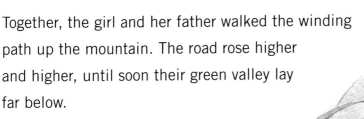

Now the path was narrow and rough with loose stones. To one side, the rocky mountain rose above them. On the other side, a steep cliff dropped down to the river. The old man couldn't hear anything above the thundering roar of the water. But his daughter suddenly stopped still, her head tilted to one side, listening.

"Quick!" She grabbed her father's arm and pulled him back, as a sudden fall of rocks crashed on to the path. The rocks landed just where they'd been standing.

Her father let out a deep breath. "You heard the rocks crumbling before they fell?" he said, amazed. And he hugged his daughter tight.

Soon the path ended and they had to scramble over huge rocks and boulders. Onwards and upwards they went, until at last they reached the great white peak of the mountain, covered in cloud.

The old man called up to the cloud. He came rumbling through the sky, his lightning eyes flashing.

The girl clung to her father's arm and trembled as she looked at the blue-black cloud. "I'm sorry," she said, "he's far too stormy for me."

The old man sighed, but he held his frightened daughter close. Then he called up to the sky once again. "Oh, dark cloud! Is there anyone on earth who's more powerful than you?"

The cloud rumbled and flashed. "More powerful than me? Why, the wind can blow me clean away. Out at sea, his storm winds are the strongest in all India. *He's* more powerful than I."

So the girl and her father travelled back down the mountain and followed the river towards the sea, where the ocean breeze blew.

As they neared the ocean, the great river turned into a maze of islands and muddy waterways. Father and daughter waded through swampy streams. "Beware," the old man said, looking at the mangrove trees on the islands with a frown, "there could be tigers or crocodiles ... "

Bumpy brown logs floated on the surface of
the water and the girl watched them with
sharp eyes. She saw one log open
its jaws. "Father!" she cried.
Quickly, she scrambled up
a tree and held out her
hand for her father
to follow.

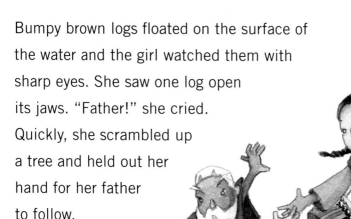

From the safety of the tree, the old
man and his daughter looked down into
the swirling water. The crocodile blinked
its eyes and slid away. Again, the old man
breathed a sigh of relief and hugged his
daughter tight. "Thank you!"

Finally, at the mouth of the river, the water flowed out to join the open sea. The girl and her father stood on the shore and he called to the wind. It came sweeping and roaring in from the ocean, whistling around them and swirling their hair around their heads. The girl shivered. She pulled her scarf close around her neck and whispered in her father's ear. "It's no good. First the wind blows one way, then the other. He isn't the right husband for me."

The old man nodded and stroked his daughter's hair. "Wild wind!" he called. "Is there anyone on earth who's more powerful than you?"

"Ohhh," breathed the wind. "How loud I howl! How cold I blow! But I can't move the great Himalaya Mountains. *They're* more powerful than me."

The old man and his daughter looked at each other. They must return to the mountain above their very own home! The old man laughed. "The best journeys are never straight! Let's return to where we started from."

So back they went, away from the shore, along the river, through the swamps, all the way home.

Finally, the old man and his daughter stood at the foot of
the mountain where their adventure had begun. But the girl
looked up to its peak and frowned. "Father," she
said, "the mountain's old and set in his ways.
He's not the right match for me."

"Well, that's that," said the old man with a heavy sigh.
He dropped his bundle to the ground and sat himself down
beside it.

The girl crouched down beside him. "I remember what you
taught me," she said. "You always said: never give up."
Then she stood up and called to the mountain herself.
"Mighty mountain! Is there anyone on earth who's more
powerful than you?"

The mountain thought long and hard. "There's only one who's more powerful than me," it boomed at last. "A creature with sharp teeth and strong claws who can nibble right through my rock-hard earth. He lives in there ... "

The old man and his daughter looked down and saw a narrow hole. Beyond it was a twisting tunnel that led deep into the centre of the mountain. They felt the chill air and heard the drip-drip-drip of cold water. They looked at each other and grinned, then crawled into the mountain.

Chapter 5

In the middle of the mountain, they found a great cave.
And in the middle of the cave, sitting on a small stone,
they found ... a little brown mouse.

"Ah," the girl sighed. "The one that can nibble
the mountain that stops the wind that scatters
the cloud that covers the sun.
The most powerful creature
in all the world!"

The brown mouse smiled at the girl. And when he smiled, his nose wrinkled and his eyes shone. The girl smiled back. "Oh yes," she said, "he's the one that calls to my heart. If only I could marry him … " Her shoulders drooped. "But a girl can't marry a mouse."

The old man was silent for a long time. At last he said, "There *is* one way you could marry him." Then he told his daughter the story of how he'd changed her from a mouse to a girl.

The girl thought for a moment, then she looked up at her father. "Will you change me back, so that I can marry the mouse? I'll still come and visit, all the time. I'll always be your daughter."

The old man took his daughter's hands in his. He looked into her shining eyes and nodded.

Then he closed his eyes and began to chant. His voice echoed around the cave, growing louder and louder until ...

He opened his eyes and there in front of him was a beautiful white mouse, her eyes shining with happiness.

The very next day the white mouse and the brown mouse were married. The sun shone and fluffy white clouds floated by on a gentle breeze, while the snow-capped mountain looked down on them all.

And before long, the old man and the old woman
had a hundred tiny mouseling grandchildren.
And they loved each and every one of them.

The most powerful of them all

Ideas for reading

Written by Clare Dowdall, PhD
Lecturer and Primary Literacy Consultant

Reading objectives:
- identify themes and conventions
- discuss their understanding and explain the meaning of words in context
- make predictions from details stated and applied

Spoken language objectives:
- participate in discussions, presentations, performances, role play, improvisations and debates

Curriculum Links: Geography – physical geography; locational knowledge

Resources: Map of the world; ICT; musical instruments for accompaniment

Build a context for reading

- Ask children if they know what the Himalayas are. Explain that they're a mountain range in Nepal, a country that borders India. Show children where this is on a map.

- Look at the front cover and help children read the title. Discuss what "the Panchatantra" might be. Explain that is a collection of folk tales from India.

- Read the blurb together. Ask children to predict what might happen to the man and his daughter on their journey to find her a husband.

Understand and apply reading strategies

- Read pp2–5 to the children. Check children's understanding by asking them to explain what is special about the old man, and what he and his wife had always wanted?

- Challenge children to predict how the couple might help the mouse. Develop their predictions by asking leading questions to help them understand that the mouse may become the child that they wish for.